Ollie's Folly

RUTH LERNER PERLE

Illustrated by Judy Blankenship

Grolier Enterprises, Inc.,   Danbury, Connecticut

Emmy
the Exaggerating
Elephant

Fenton
the Fearful Frog

Gertie
the Grungy Goat

Herbie
the Happy
Hamster

Ivy
the Impatient
Iguana

Ollie
the Obedient
Ostrich

Perry
the Polite
Porcupine

Queenie
the Quiet Quail

Rupert
the Resourceful
Rhinoceros

Wendy
the Wise
Woodchuck

Xavier
the X ploring
Xenops

Yori
the Yucky Yak

Ziggy
the Zippy Zebra

NOTE TO PARENTS

Ollie's Folly
A story about obeying rules

In this story, Ollie the Obedient Ostrich's experience demonstrates that it pays to follow rules and obey laws. When some of the AlphaPets tease him for being a "goody-two-shoes", Ollie feels embarrassed and decides to change his ways. He flaunts several health and safety rules with disastrous results. In the end, all the AlphaPets realize just how important rules can be.

In addition to enjoying this story with your child, you can use it to teach a gentle lesson about the importance of rules and warning signs. At the same time, this story deals with the problem of teasing, and emphasizes how essential it is to do what you know is right—despite what others say or do. You might also want to explain the word *folly* as a foolish action that may result in unexpected consequences.

You can also use this story to introduce the letter **O**. As you read about Ollie the Obedient Ostrich, ask your child to listen for all the words that start with **O** and point to the objects that begin with **O**. Explain that the vowel **O** makes several different sounds. When you've finished reading the story, your child will enjoy doing the activity at the end of the book.

The AlphaPets™ characters were conceived and created by Ruth Lerner Perle.
Characters interpreted and designed by Deborah Colvin Borgo.
Cover/book design and production by Norton & Company.
Logo design by Deborah Colvin Borgo and Nancy S. Norton.
Printed and Manufactured in the United States of America

One wintry day, as Ollie the Obedient Ostrich was on his way to Harriet's Heavenly Hamburger Hut, he met Ivy the Impatient Iguana and Nelly the Naughty Newt in front of the bookstore.

Just as Ollie was about to say hello, Nelly whispered something in Ivy's ear and they both laughed.

"What's the joke?" Ollie asked.

"Oh, nothing!" Nelly said, and she started to giggle.

"You look really funny wearing those big boots and carrying your umbrella," said Ivy.

"But the weather reporter said it was going to storm today and to take our umbrellas," Ollie explained.

"Well, it's not storming, and you look silly," Nelly said.

Ollie looked down at his clothes. "Maybe I do look silly," he thought.

Ollie felt embarrassed, but he continued walking down the street. When he came to the corner, the traffic light was red, so he stopped.

"What are you waiting for, silly?" Ivy called.

"You're supposed to cross only at the green light!" Ollie said. "There may be some cars coming, and you could get hit." But Ivy and Nelly started to cross the street anyway.

"Why waste time standing at the corner when there *aren't* any cars coming?" Ivy said. She laughed and skipped across the street with Nelly.

When Ollie arrived at Harriet's Hamburger Hut, he saw Justin the Joking Jackal having lunch with Gertie the Grungy Goat.

Ollie waved to them, and then stood in line waiting for his turn to order. When he got his hamburger, onion rings and orange soda, Ollie carried his tray to Justin's table.

"Hi, everybody," Ollie said. "May I sit with you?"

"Sure, Ollie," Justin said, blowing bubbles in his soda.

"You can sit next to me," Gertie said. "Don't mind the mess."

Ollie sat down, placed a napkin in his lap, and started eating his lunch.

When they were finished eating, Gertie and Justin got up to leave.

"Hey! What about your trash?" Ollie said. "The sign says we should clear the table!"

"I never pay attention to signs," Gertie said. "I came here to eat, not clean!"

"But, but . . ." Ollie said.

"Oh, Ollie! Don't be such a goody-two-shoes!" teased Gertie.

"You mean goody-snowboots, don't you?" Justin shouted, and started to laugh.

Ollie felt his face turn hot, and his heart started to pound. He cleared the table and then he hurried home.

Ollie was really upset by the time he got to his house. He ran into his room, threw himself on his bed and wept.

"I always try to do the right things, but it's no use," he cried. "Everybody makes fun of me."

Ollie got up and punched his pillow. "Maybe they're right!" he shouted. "I'm tired of following rules and doing what I'm told. Things are going to be different from now on! No more Mr. Obedient! I'm not doing what I should do—ever, ever again!"

That evening, Ollie decided *not* to have vegetables for supper. Instead, he ate three bags of potato chips and two boxes of chocolate cookies.

He did *not* brush his teeth before he went to bed.

He did *not* hang up his clothes.

He did *not* go to sleep at the usual time. He stayed up and watched TV.

The next morning, Ollie was awakened by the ringing of the telephone.

It was Wendy the Wise Woodchuck. "Good morning, Ollie," she said. "It's ten o'clock. I've been waiting for you for a long time. We're supposed to go skating this morning. Did you forget?"

"I guess I overslept," Ollie said, rubbing his eyes. "I went to sleep late last night."

"That's not like you," Wendy said. "Is there something wrong?"

"No, I'm fine," Ollie said. "Go ahead without me, I'll meet you at the skating pond."

Ollie hung up the phone and got out of bed. But he *wasn't* fine. He was tired from staying up so late. His tummy hurt from all the junk food he had eaten the night before. And his mouth felt funny from not brushing his teeth before going to bed.

Ollie looked for his shoes and belt, but he couldn't find them. It took him forever to get dressed.

"Oh, dear," Ollie thought to himself. "I wish I had had more sleep, brushed my teeth, and prepared my clothes for today. It's no fun feeling like this."

Ollie went to the kitchen to make himself some breakfast. He prepared sliced oranges, a bowl of oatmeal, and a cheese and tomato omelette. He set the table neatly and sat down. But just as he was about to start eating, he remembered . . . No more Mr. Obedient! Ollie jumped up and threw his napkin down.

"No breakfast for me today!" he shouted.

Ollie grabbed his skates, ran out of the house, and slammed the door behind him.

When Ollie arrived at the skating pond, many of the AlphaPets were already there. Ivy and Nelly were having a race, Justin was skating backwards, and Gertie was twirling with Wendy.

Wendy waved to Ollie. "Hey, Ollie! Hurry!" she called, "We've been waiting for you!"

DANGER
THIN ICE
KEEP OFF

Ollie laced his skates and skated out onto the pond.

There was a sign on one side of the ice that said

DANGER THIN ICE KEEP OFF

Ollie was about to circle around to the other side of the pond. But then he saw the AlphaPets watching him.

"I'm sure everybody expects me to obey that sign and go around the long way," Ollie said to himself. "I'll show them all how fast I can get there! I'll skate right past that silly old sign. No more Mr. Obedient for me!"

Ollie took a deep breath and skated right past the sign.

Then, suddenly, *CRACK!* The ice started to break and water came seeping up through the cracks! Ollie tried to skate away, but wherever he went there were more and more cracks. Poor Ollie! He slipped and almost fell through the ice!

DANGER
THIN ICE
KEEP OFF

"Help! Help!" he cried.

"We're coming!" shouted the AlphaPets.

Bradley the Brave Bear rushed over and threw Ollie an oar. Then all the AlphaPets helped pull him to safety.

The AlphaPets helped Ollie to a bench, and wrapped a blanket around his shoulders.

Ollie shivered, so everyone gathered closely around him to keep him warm. "Oh, Ollie, whatever made you ignore that sign?" Wendy asked.

"I didn't want you to make fun of me!" Ollie whispered.

Then Ivy said, "We feel terrible, Ollie. We were wrong to make fun of you for following rules, and we're sorry."

Wendy gave Ollie a big hug and said, "It's not always fun to obey the rules, but now we all know that it can be a lot less fun *not* to pay attention to them."

"Yes," agreed Ollie as he patted his empty tummy. "And I also know that I'm starving! I shouldn't have skipped breakfast."

Bradley looked at his watch. "It's almost noon. I guess we're all getting hungry. Let's go have a bite to eat."

"Yippee!" shouted the AlphaPets. They changed into their shoes and then walked back to town. And when they came to the corner—no one crossed until the light turned green.

Please listen to me and learn these words.

oatmeal

orange

oboe

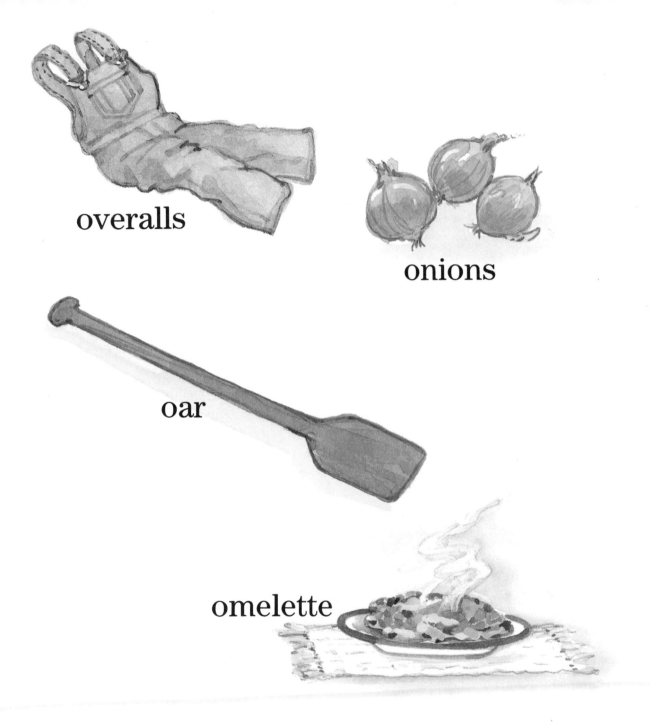

overalls

onions

oar

omelette

Look back at the story and try to find these and other words that begin with O.

Know Your Alphabet

Aa Bb

Gg Hh

Mm Nn Oo Pp

Uu Vv Ww